This edition published by Parragon Books Ltd in 2015

Parragon Books Ltd
Chartist House
15–17 Trim Street
Bath BA1 1HA, UK
www.parragon.com

ISBN 978-1-4723-4944-6

Printed in China

Disney · PIXAR

THE GOOD DINOSAUR

PaRragon

Bath · New York · Cologne · Melbourne · Delhi
Hong Kong · Shenzhen · Singapore · Amsterdam

A long time ago, dinosaurs ruled the earth. These giant creatures were wiped out when an asteroid crashed into our planet. But what if the asteroid had missed and the dinosaurs had survived?

In a world where dinosaurs became farmers instead of extinct, there lived two Apatosauruses called Henry and Ida. They loved each other very much and decided to start a family.

Henry and Ida had three children. Buck and Libby were both strong and confident dinosaurs. But their brother, Arlo, was small for an Apatosaurus.

From the moment he hatched, Arlo was a small, scared little guy. He was frightened of everything – even doing his chores! Most of all, Arlo was scared of the wilderness that lay beyond the fence. He only felt safe in his home, on the farm by Clawtooth Mountain.

One night, Henry took
Arlo into a field on the farm.
An insect landed on Arlo's nose
and the little dinosaur cried out
when he saw the bug close up –
it seemed huge and threatening.
Henry told his son to stand still
and then blew gently on the bug.
It glowed. It was a firefly!

Arlo looked at his Poppa
and smiled.

Suddenly, Poppa swept his tail
through the grass and hundreds
of glowing fireflies flew up
into the sky! Arlo gasped in
amazement. They were beautiful.

Arlo felt safe with his Poppa.

The next day, Henry discovered that a critter had broken into the farm and eaten some of their corn.

"I've got a job for you," he told Arlo. "YOU are gonna catch that critter!"

Arlo was afraid, but he wanted to make his Poppa proud.

"I'll take care of that critter, Poppa," he said. "It won't stand a chance."

Arlo waited by the trap that he and his Poppa had built until he heard something struggling inside. He got his first look at the critter – it was a human boy! The dinosaur was scared to hurt the critter, so he released it into the wilderness.

Henry wasn't pleased when he saw the empty trap. He decided
to teach his son to overcome his fear by taking him on a critter hunt.
Arlo was scared. What if they got lost?

"We can follow the river home," Henry told him.

They searched the wilderness for the critter, but before long
a terrifying storm set in. The rain caused the river to overflow and
poor Henry was swept away by the water. Arlo was devastated –
he would never see his Poppa again.

With Poppa gone, the family had to work very hard to keep their farm going. Arlo's Momma was worn out. One day, as she carried a huge load of corn on her back, she stumbled.

Arlo ran to her. "You need to rest," he said.

"If we don't get this harvest in before the first snow," Momma told Arlo, "we won't have enough food for winter."

Arlo wanted to help. He picked up the load of corn and carried it for his mother.

"Don't worry," he said. "I won't let us starve."

As Arlo began to load corn into the farm's huge silo, he spotted the critter he had set free! It was stealing corn again.

Desperate to finish the job his Poppa had given him, Arlo wrestled with the critter. But as they fought they tumbled backwards and fell into the river! By the time Arlo came up for air, the river's current had swept him away from the farm.

"Momma, Momma!" he cried, but he was too far away to be heard.

Then *BAM!* The little dinosaur banged his head on a rock and he was pulled under by the current.

When Arlo woke up, he had no idea where he was. His head and legs hurt, and he was alone. He had landed on a small strip of sand surrounded by huge cliffs. There was no way out!

He struggled to his feet and tried to climb one of the steep cliffs, but he slipped. Just then, he heard a strange howl. He looked up ... and standing on the clifftop above him was the critter.

"You!" Arlo shouted angrily. "This is all your fault!"

But the critter didn't react. It just calmly sat and watched.

"Get over here!" said Arlo, using his long neck to reach the top of the cliff and gnash his teeth at the boy. The boy did as he was told and jumped on to Arlo's nose.

"Argh!" screamed Arlo, terrified. "Get away!"

The boy jumped off Arlo's nose and disappeared.

With the critter gone, Arlo managed to climb the cliff. At the top, he took a breath and looked around. The wilderness seemed endless – there were mountains and forests as far as the eye could see.

"Where's home?" Arlo asked himself.

He looked down at the river and suddenly remembered something his Poppa had said. He could follow the river all the way home!

Arlo set out on his long walk home along the river, but before long he started to feel hungry. He balanced himself on a large rock and tried to reach some juicy berries high up in a tree. Just then, the rock slipped and Arlo fell!

Arlo tried to pick himself up, but realized his foot was stuck between some rocks. No matter how hard he tried, he couldn't free himself.

Soon, darkness fell. Arlo could hear strange noises all around him. He wasn't safe out here! He curled up into a ball and tried to block out the scary sounds of the wilderness.

The next morning, Arlo awoke with a start. For a moment he wasn't sure where he was, then he remembered.

He looked down at his foot – it was free! Someone had pushed the rocks away and there were tracks in the mud around him.

Arlo continued on his way, but it soon began to rain.

Arlo decided to build a shelter using twigs and branches.

Little forest creatures peeked out of their homes to watch him at work. Arlo, who had never built anything in his life, was sure they were laughing at him.

Suddenly, Arlo heard rustling in the bushes – something was coming towards him! He panted with fear as the creature finally appeared....

It was the critter!

"You again!" cried Arlo. "Get outta here!"

The boy looked at Arlo and ran back into the bushes. He reappeared a moment later carrying an armful of berries. He dropped them in front of the dinosaur. Arlo was unsure what to do at first, but he was so hungry he couldn't resist. He ate the whole lot!

"Thank you," said Arlo. "I'm still going to squeeze the life out of you ... but could you find me some more?"

The boy took off into the forest, sniffing the ground. Arlo followed
him and soon the boy stopped in his tracks and tapped his foot.
He'd found something. Berries! Arlo ran towards the berries, but the
boy suddenly jumped in front of him and growled.

"What's with you?" Arlo asked. "Crazy critter."

Arlo broke off a branch of berries to eat, and a huge snake fell on to his face!

"Aaghhhh!" Arlo screamed, flinging the snake to the ground.

The snake rose up in front of Arlo, but the boy jumped in front of him once again. As the snake lunged towards them, the boy darted out of the way, then crept up behind the reptile and head-butted it! The snake wriggled away into the forest.

Arlo was very grateful to the boy
for protecting him against the snake.
Maybe this critter wasn't so bad after all.
"Hello," came a voice.
Arlo jumped at the sound. The boy wasn't
bothered – he rummaged in a bush nearby.
The voice belonged to a Styracosaurus,
who was hidden in the trees. His horns were
covered with lots of tiny forest animals!

The stranger spoke again. "That boy protected you. Why?"

"I-I don't know," Arlo stuttered.

"Hmm," said the stranger. "I name him, I keep him." He wanted to take the boy for himself!

The stranger closed his eyes and began to call out names to the boy. Arlo joined in, realizing he didn't want to lose his companion.

"Squirt!" Arlo called, but the boy ignored him. Then he tried again – "Spot!" The boy turned round, looked at Arlo and ran over to him.

"He is named," said the Styracosaurus. "That creature will keep you safe. Don't ever lose him."

Arlo and Spot spent the rest of the day finding food and playing together. As night fell, Arlo thought of his home.

"I miss my family," he said. But Spot didn't understand.

Arlo found some sticks and made dinosaur shapes on the ground. The shapes were Poppa, Momma, Buck and Libby.

Spot made some stick shapes of his own. This was *his* family.

The boy pushed dirt over the stick people, and Arlo realized that meant Spot's family had died. Arlo turned his Poppa stick shape over.

"I miss him," he said.

Spot patted Arlo's leg to comfort him, and then the boy looked up to the moon and let out a sad howl. Arlo placed his paw on his Poppa shape and joined in. The new friends howled into the night.

The next morning, the sky was dark – a storm was coming.
The pair started to make their way along the river, but Arlo was nervous.
    "We should stop!" he called. But Spot couldn't hear him over the wind.
BOOM! Thunder crashed overhead. Arlo couldn't help but think
of the day he lost his Poppa. He ran away from the storm in a panic and
hid in the roots of a huge tree.

Finally, the storm passed. Spot sniffed around for Arlo and found him curled up in a ball underneath the tree. Arlo crawled out from his shelter and looked around.

"Wh-where's the river?" he asked, getting scared. "I've lost the river!"

Arlo tried to ask some passing Pterodactyls for help, but they turned out to be nasty and wanted to eat Spot! Arlo and Spot ran away, right into ...

... two T. rexes!

"Agh!" Arlo yelled.

But the T. rexes were on Arlo and Spot's side. They easily fought off the Pterodactyls, and then one of them turned to Arlo.

"Hey, you okay, kid?" said the T. rex, whose name was Nash.

"Y-y-yes," stammered Arlo.

Another T. rex, called Ramsey, looked at Spot.
"Well, ain't you the cutest little thing?"
she said as Spot leaned against her leg.

"He likes you," said Arlo.

Just then, a third, larger T. rex
arrived. This was Butch. "You got
no business being out here,"
he told Arlo.

"Yes, sir," Arlo replied.
"I'm trying to get home,
but I lost the river."

Arlo asked the T. rexes if they could help him find the river that led to Clawtooth Mountain – his home. But Butch explained they had just lost their herd of longhorns and they had to find them.

"We can't help ya, kid," Butch told Arlo.

Arlo started thinking. "Wait," he said, "but what if *we* could help *you?*"

Butch stopped in his tracks and Arlo continued. "Spot can sniff out anything! I seen him do it!"

Arlo and the T. rexes made a deal.
If Arlo and Spot could help them
find their herd, the T. rexes
would show the pair the
direction of the river.

"Come on, Spot," said Arlo. "Sniff it out, boy."

Arlo and the T. rexes took tiny steps behind little Spot as he sniffed the ground. It was slow work.

"If you're pullin' my leg, I'm gonna eat yours," Butch told Arlo.

Arlo chuckled nervously. Then he dug his nose into the ground and scooped up Spot.

"We gotta go faster," he whispered to the boy.

Arlo lowered his head to the ground, with Spot still sitting on the end of his nose. They moved along like this as the boy sniffed for tracks.

Soon Spot saw something on the ground – longhorn tracks! The group followed the tracks over a ridge, and there was the herd.

Butch told everyone to wait. He knew it wasn't safe – there were rustlers out there who wanted to steal the longhorns.

"I've got a job for you," Butch said to Arlo.

"I'm not real good at jobs...." Arlo replied.

Butch wanted Arlo to make a noise to draw out the rustlers. Arlo was keen to help, so he nervously stepped out into the field with Spot on his back.

Arlo opened his mouth and tried to yell, but nothing came out!
He was trying very hard to get over his fear. He opened his mouth
again, but he still couldn't make a sound.

Suddenly, Spot bit Arlo on the leg!

"Aaaaghhh!" Arlo screamed.

One by one, the rustlers – who were scary-looking Raptors –
emerged from the grass, making their
way towards Arlo.

Arlo froze in terror. He was sure
that this was the end....

At that moment, Butch leaped out of the grass and grabbed one of the Raptors. Nash and Ramsey arrived and fought off the others.

Then the herd of longhorns began to charge – right at Arlo! The little dinosaur was frozen in fear. Spot knew he had to help his friend, so he jumped on to Arlo's back and gave him a nudge. Arlo ran and hid behind a huge boulder, protecting them both.

Butch appeared nearby, still fighting a Raptor. Arlo and Spot watched as the Raptor got the upper hand and pinned Butch to the ground!

"Nab his tail!" Butch called to Arlo. Arlo just shivered, but Spot nudged him again in the neck. The dinosaur burst into life and charged straight at the Raptor, head-butting it across the field!

"Aaghhh!" yelled Arlo. He couldn't believe it – he had done it!

That night, Arlo and Spot joined their new T. rex friends round a campfire.

"You and that critter showed real grit today," Butch told Arlo.

The three T. rexes told stories about when they had fought off other beasts – even crocodiles!

Arlo was amazed. "I'm done being scared," he said.

"Who said I'm not scared?" said Butch.

Arlo was surprised. "But you fought off that croc—"

"Listen, kid," Butch continued, "you can't get rid of fear. But you can get through it. You can find out what you're made of."

Just then, something drifted down from the sky. It was snow! That meant winter was coming.

"I gotta get home to Momma," Arlo said.

"A deal's a deal," said Butch. "At first light, we ride."

The T. rexes showed Arlo and Spot the way to the river and then said their goodbyes. The boy and the dinosaur were on their way again. They played and laughed together as they ran along.

Soon, they came to the top of a hill and Spot signalled to Arlo to lift his head up through the clouds. The dinosaur did as he was told and the pair gasped at the beautiful view.

"Wow," said Arlo.

They could see Clawtooth Mountain – they were heading home! The two of them watched the sunset and felt truly happy.

The next day, as Arlo and Spot rounded a bend, Clawtooth Mountain came into view.

"It's so close," said Arlo. "We're almost there, Spot!"

Arlo lifted his head and howled in excitement. Spot joined in and suddenly another howl came back in response. Spot and Arlo saw the figure of a human man on the ridge ahead.

Spot jumped from Arlo's back and carefully made his way towards the man. As Spot got further and further away, Arlo started to worry that the little critter might leave him. The dinosaur quickly caught up with Spot and scooped him up on to his back.

"We need to get home," Arlo said, heading off on the trail.

As the pair continued, the river trail moved into the mountains. Thunder rumbled overhead once more, the wind picked up and it began to rain. Arlo's feet started to sink into the wet ground and he found it hard to keep walking.

Before Arlo knew what was happening, the Pterodactyls appeared in the sky above them. They swooped down and one of them caught hold of Spot!

"No!" Arlo yelled, trying to grab the boy back. But the Pterodactyl was too strong. With one last tug, the creature took to the sky with Spot grasped in its claws.

"Spot!" Arlo cried as his little friend disappeared.

Luckily, Spot managed to break away from the
Pterodactyl's grasp and hide himself inside a tree trunk.
He was hurt and the Pterodactyls were smashing into
the tree over and over again, trying to grab hold of him.
Meanwhile, the storm overhead was getting worse.
Spot howled and heard a return cry close by.
Then, suddenly ...

... Arlo appeared! He had come to save his friend.

Arlo charged at the Pterodactyls and head-butted one of them into the river. Next, as the storm raged around him, he uprooted a huge tree with his tail and smashed it into the other Pterodactyls.

Spot cried out from his tree trunk – he was stuck fast. The ground had begun to tremble and Arlo realized that a flash flood was racing towards them.

Suddenly, Spot's tree trunk was uprooted by the rising river and he was quickly carried away by the current. Arlo reached for the boy, but it was no use. Meanwhile, the flash flood was approaching – there was a wall of water heading straight towards Spot. Arlo had to reach him – now!

The little dinosaur ran faster than he'd ever run before, trying to catch up with Spot and outrun the flood.

Once Arlo was in line with Spot's tree, he gathered all his strength and leaped. He reached out for Spot, but the wall of water hit Arlo in mid-air and knocked him down into the river.

Arlo struggled to swim against the river's fast current. The rapids were pulling him under.

"Spot!" he yelled.

Suddenly, he caught sight of Spot, still crouched inside the tree trunk. Then, over the noise of the river, he heard the loud rushing of a waterfall!

Arlo used all his strength to swim towards Spot. The boy broke free from the tree, jumped into the water and began swimming towards Arlo. Just as the two friends reached each other, they dropped over the edge....

The pair fell a long way and splashed into the water at the bottom of the waterfall. After a moment, Arlo appeared on the surface of the water holding Spot. The dinosaur climbed on to dry land and held his little friend.

Arlo and Spot looked at each other and smiled. They were feeling shocked and bruised, but they were okay.

The next morning, after a good night's rest, Arlo and Spot awoke to find that the storm had passed. They set off once more on the trail through the mountains and along the river.

Soon, they heard a familiar howl. Up ahead stood the man they had seen the day before. This time, there was an entire human family with him! The humans made their way out of the woods and Spot ran over to them.

Arlo watched as the family gathered around Spot. He knew what had to be done.

When Spot came running back over to Arlo, the dinosaur gently pushed Spot back towards the family.

Spot didn't understand.

Arlo pushed him again and then drew a circle in the ground around Spot and the humans. Spot knew what Arlo was saying.

As Spot hugged Arlo goodbye, both friends had tears in their eyes. They had been through so much together. They were best friends, but they knew it would be better for Spot to live with a family of humans.

Arlo walked the last part of his journey alone. Finally, the farm came into view and Arlo saw his Momma.

"Arlo!" cried Momma as she spotted her son.

Buck and Libby came running towards them and the family laughed and hugged. Arlo was home at last.